Richie Ochoa is a new author from Southern California. He recently decided to write his first children's book after having his first child. He hopes that through his writing he will entertain both children and parents alike, as they both might relate to his stories. Richie hopes that his books will also encourage others to take chances, follow their dreams, and see where they end.

# The Grumpy Little TOAD

## Richie Ochoa

AUSTIN MACAULEY PUBLISHERS™

LONDON * CAMBRIDGE * NEW YORK * SHARJAH

# Copyright © Richie Ochoa (2019)

**Ordering Information:**

Quantity sales: special discounts are available on quantity purchases by corporations, associations, and others. For details, contact the publisher at the address below.

**Publisher's Cataloging-in-Publication data**
Ochoa, Richie
The Grumpy Little Toad

ISBN 9781645361817 (Paperback)
ISBN 9781645361824 (Hardback)
ISBN 9781645366058 (ePub e-book)

Library of Congress Control Number: 2019917413

The main category of the book — JUVENILE FICTION / Animals / Frogs & Toads

www.austinmacauley.com/us

First Published (2019)
Austin Macauley Publishers LLC
40 Wall Street, 28th Floor
New York, NY 10005
USA
mail-usa@austinmacauley.com
+1 (646) 5125767

To Blake and Amanda for our early mornings and sleepless nights. I wouldn't trade them for the world.

A field, a pond, a lily pad, and on top,
three toads: a mom, a dad,
And snuggled there warm in between,
something new, small, and green.

6

This new arrival: a ball of joy, a happy,
hoppy baby boy.
When nighttime fell, they went to bed,
unaware of what lay ahead.

Every hour almost on the dot, the little
toad whined and started to hop.
He whined when hungry and when he was wet,
When his tummy was rumbly, he was always upset.

Sometimes he was fed and he seemed to be dry,
They had no clue why he started to cry.

So they cuddled up close with a big family hug,
And the toad fell asleep, all he wanted was love.
Now the little one slept and Mom and Dad closed their eyes
As others around them woke up and the sun did rise.

With the new light of day, the little toad woke.
He hopped on his parents with a good morning croak.

And through half-open eyes after
a night without sleep,

18

The two stared at the toad with his smile
cheek to cheek

So with love in their hearts, they arose to the day,
Filled with laughing and cuddling, napping and play.

Till the sun went to bed and the three snuggled in,
Kisses goodnight, warm hugs, and grins.
After a day on the go and a night without end,
They lovingly prepared to do it again.

CPSIA information can be obtained
at www.ICGtesting.com
Printed in the USA
LVHW071102261219
641447LV00022B/558/P